OTHER BOOKS ABOUT SEBASTIAN

Mary Blount Christian

SEBASTIAN
(Super Sleuth)
and the Flying Elephant

Illustrated by Lisa McCue

Simon & Schuster Books for Young Readers

Remembering Winifred Perry,

who enjoyed a good laugh

—M. B. C.

SIMON & SCHUSTER BOOKS FOR YOUNG READERS
An imprint of Simon & Schuster Children's Publishing Division
1230 Avenue of the Americas
New York, New York 10020
Text copyright © 1994 by Mary Blount Christian
Illustrations copyright © 1994 by Lisa McCue
Simon & Schuster Books for Young Readers is a trademark of Simon & Schuster
Printed in the United States of America

10   9   8   7   6   5   4   3   2

The text of this book is set in 12 point Primer.
The illustrations are rendered in scratchboard.

LIBRARY OF CONGRESS CATALOGING-IN-PUBLICATION DATA
Christian, Mary Blount.
Sebastian, (super sleuth) and the flying elephant /
Mary Blount Christian ; illustrated by Lisa McCue. — 1st ed.
p.   cm. — (Sebastian, super sleuth)
Summary: When Detective John Quincy Jones is told to find the
circus's missing elephant by nightfall, his faithful canine
companion must come to the rescue as usual.
ISBN 0-02-718252-5
[1. Dogs—Fiction.   2. Circus—Fiction.   3. Mystery
and detective stories.]   I. McCue, Lisa, ill.
II. Title.   III. Series: Christian, Mary Blount.
Sebastian, super sleuth.
PZ7.C4528Sdf   1994
[Fic—dc20]   94-14434

Contents

1
Right on Track

Sebastian ignored John's sharp command to heel and squirmed his way to the front of the crowd. He was too excited to remain at the rear. For weeks he had seen the show bills posted around town advertising the circus. He would not miss its arrival.

Suddenly, Sebastian's supersensitive paws picked up the ground vibrations of an approaching train. First the shiny black engine came into view, then the lipstick red cars decorated with gold letters: BODOLINI'S GREATEST LITTLE BIG TOP SHOW IN THE WORLD. Bigger-than-life pictures showed leaping lions, snarling tigers, and brightly costumed people swinging on trapezes or balanced in a human pyramid.

Sebastian wiggled excitedly. This was the first human circus he had ever seen. Once, in a shopping mall, he saw a flea circus. However, performing fleas, even if they could do somersaults and play catch with tiny balls, did not appeal to this canine cop.

Detectives in a large city filled with crime, Sebastian and John needed cheery diversions once in a while. Actually, only John—John Quincy Jones, Sebastian's human—was an official cop on the payroll. Yet his four-on-the-floor buddy, Sebastian (Super Sleuth), solved all the crimes, thereby saving John's job and assuring himself a steady supply of burgers and meaty tidbits.

Just as John, his fiancée, Maude Culpepper, and her Old English sheepdog, Lady Sharon, caught up with Sebastian, the crowd surged forward. Sebastian had to scramble to avoid being trampled. He was separated once again from his human. But why worry? John could take care of himself—Sebastian hoped.

Men in coveralls and heavy work boots clambered one after another from the train, shouting orders and setting up ramps. Tigers roared, monkeys quarreled, dogs barked, and horses whinnied.

A six-piece band in cadet blue jackets stepped forward. When one of them signaled, the others played "The Elephant Walk."

The doors of the first train car slid open, and an elephant emerged. Over ten feet high, she wore a bright pink tutu around her massive gray body and a headdress of sequins and dyed ostrich plumes. She looked just like the elephant on their show bills. Her trunk, legs, and face were painted with bright designs. A heavy metal band encircled one of her pillarlike legs.

Her tusks, Sebastian recalled, were actually elongated incisor teeth. They were tipped with silver knobs but still looked dangerous.

Judging from the size and shape of her ears, the length of her trunk, and the dip in her back, she was an African elephant. They were once believed to be the most difficult to train. But Belgian farmers discovered that if you began training them in their youth (when they were a mere six hundred pounds or so) and treated them kindly, they learned as well as the Asiatic variety.

At the foot of the ramp, a man in a gold-trimmed green jumpsuit tapped the elephant's chest with his stick and shouted, "Up, Tahsha, up!"

The elephant rose on her back legs. She lifted her long trunk and gave a mighty trumpet—something like high C—then dropped to all four feet.

The crowd cheered and clapped. A man in a red

frock coat and black top hat held a megaphone to his lips. "Folks, that's amazing Tahsha, the greatest performing elephant in the world! She waltzes, she hulas, she stands on her head. She rests her six tons atop a human so gently that she does no damage. The amazing Tahsha! That's all the show you get for free," he said.

He pointed north. "The big top will be two blocks that way. Our spectacular performances begin day after tomorrow. Any of you boys and girls who carry water to our animals will get a free ticket."

Workers rolled huge cages off the train from flatbed cars. Although canvas covered the sides of the cages, growling, rumbling noises left no doubt that these cages held the tigers and bears. The men hooked the cages together trainlike behind a tractor.

With the perky little band in the lead, the parade of cages, costumed performers, and spectators made its way to the vacant lot inside a tall fence.

Already workers were spreading a massive canvas tent over the area and erecting the poles that would keep it in place. Their huge sledgehammers drove stakes deep into the ground. Quickly the men attached ropes and guide wires to tractors at opposite ends of the tent. On a signal, the tractors pulled.

The men wrapped the ropes and wires expertly around the stakes. In what seemed only a short time, the big top took on recognizable form.

Meanwhile, boys and girls scrambled to fill buckets of water and carry them to the animals.

Sebastian sat on his haunches, waiting for his bucket to fill, then made his way to the elephant. She no longer wore her costume. Instead she wore a heavy chain attached to her ankle band, sort of an elephant handcuff staked to the ground.

From deep inside Tahsha's tummy rose a rumbling sound. Sebastian had read about that. People once believed this was digestion noise, since elephants' diets include tree branches, grass, and the like. Then scientists discovered that it is really a catlike purring that elephants and other pachyderms make when they are out of sight of their kind.

When elephants sense danger, they stop this purring. Their silence warns the others. That made a lot more sense than sounding a warning and revealing one's position to a predator. Elephants must be *almost* as smart as this sleuth hound.

Tahsha's keeper had traded his own fancy costume for more practical blue jeans. He was scrubbing the paint off the huge beast. Finished, he gently rubbed Tahsha's trunk and spoke softly to her. "It's okay, old girl. I know you miss Omar. Poor old lonely girl. Don't worry. Everything is going to be all right. Trust me."

The elephant wrapped her hoselike trunk around the man's neck in something similar to an affectionate hug.

Sebastian set down the bucket. The man pulled off his cap and scratched his thin halo of gray hair. "Well, I'll be," he said. He reached down and rubbed Sebastian under the chin. "How nice of you to bring Tahsha a drink of water. She won't forget your kind deed, pooch. Elephants never forget, you know."

Sebastian spread his lips into a panting grin. He used to think that an elephant's super memory was only mythical, like the huge beast's being afraid of mice. That is, until he'd read an article in one of the newspapers that John put under his breakfast dish. (As if he would allow a single morsel of food to drop onto the floor.)

The article had said that an elephant in India had been badly mistreated by her owner. Years later a new owner had ridden the gentle beast into the village. Spotting her former owner in the bazaar, the elephant calmly had filled her trunk and thoroughly soaked the startled man.

"Sebastian!" John said. "There you are, naughty dog. We've been looking everywhere for you."

Sebastian trotted off at John's heels. Glancing back at Tahsha, he thought what a sad-looking creature she was. The largest living mammal to walk the earth, yet she was as dependent on human kindness as a gerbil in a cage—or a dog on a leash.

The next morning, Sebastian snacked on creamy beef slices as John was drinking a leisurely cup of coffee and reading the paper.

The phone rang, and John punched the speaker button. Immediately Sebastian recognized the grouchy, grumbling voice of Chief, John's boss and Sebastian's sworn enemy. He cocked an ear, eavesdropping.

"I'm canceling everyone's day off. I need every available man and woman—even you," Chief said. "Besides the usual run of crime, the city has had a couple of weird incidents overnight."

"What happened, Chief?"

"Last night some people tried to break into the zoo. The watchman ran them off before they could get inside. Then this morning, the owner of that circus reported a missing elephant. I figured even *you* can find something that big!"

John winced visibly. "I appreciate your confidence, Chief."

"The circus has a private performance tonight for children who can't afford to buy tickets. I want that elephant there by then, or you'll be back walking a beat on the wharf."

2

Ta-ta, Tahsha

"How can anything the size of an elephant up and disappear?" John muttered as he searched for matching socks and a necktie without gravy stains.

John had no sooner dressed than the doorbell rang. It was the exterminator.

"Oh, rats!" John said.

"Rats?" the man said. "I thought I was here to exterminate fleas. I brought the wrong chemicals."

"Oh, yes," John said, "it's fleas. I just forgot you were coming. Well, there's nothing to do but take Sebastian with me. Otherwise he'll do one of his famous Houdini escapes and go on a garbage-scavenging, feline-terrorizing rampage."

John just didn't understand that it was Sebastian's duty to recycle leftovers that the neighbors so thoughtlessly discarded. As for scaring cats, this typical doggie trait was the best disguise for an under-cover canine cop.

When they arrived, the red-and-white-striped circus tent was fully erected. It was about three stories tall and as big as the police station. A large pennant bearing the name of the circus flew from its center pole. Between the fence and the big top were a number of tents, each with its own sign: RINGTOSS, FISH FOR PRIZES, GYPSY FORTUNE-TELLER, and more.

The cagey canine lifted his sensitive nose into the air and inhaled deeply. *Ahhh.* Peanuts, popcorn, caramel-coated apples, hot dogs, and other goodies were already being prepared for tonight's private performance.

The crack and thud of hammers rose from the big top, and Sebastian peeked inside. The workmen were setting up the tiered bleachers, where the audience would sit. The nets and trapeze riggings were up. The grip, the man who handled the electrical equipment, was testing colored spotlights on them.

A middle-aged man wearing coveralls and a pained expression rushed forward. He shook John's hand. Sebastian recognized him from last night.

"I'm Nick Bodolini," he said. "I own this circus.

You have got to find Tahsha. Without her, there *is* no circus." He pulled a red bandanna from his back pocket and wiped his ruddy face. "Besides, I'm fond of the old girl; I don't want anything to happen to her."

Sebastian shuddered. Eccentric collectors would pay anything to own a rare, endangered beast. Some unscrupulous people would kill her just for her beautiful ivory tusks. They would make lamps and ashtrays of her massive legs and feet, and boots and purses from her hide.

John glanced around the area. "This isn't far from the center of the city. People are pretty blasé, but I think they'd notice an elephant lumbering around the streets. It isn't far from some wooded areas, either. Perhaps she smelled vegetation, and it reminded her of the jungle."

Mr. Bodolini shook his head vigorously. "We closed the gates last night. We posted guards at the gates. After all, we don't want outsiders wandering among our animals."

"None of the guards saw her when she escaped?" John asked.

"She didn't escape! She was kidnapped!" Mr. Bodolini insisted. "Follow me; I'll show you."

"Have you received a ransom note or any threatening calls?" John asked.

"The phone isn't connected yet," Mr. Bodolini said. "And I haven't received any notes."

A man and woman led past them six brown horses with identical white spots on their foreheads and white legs that looked like stockings. "Any news yet?" the man asked.

Mr. Bodolini waved them off.

Sebastian and John followed Mr. Bodolini through the maze of campers and tents that were the living quarters for the circus performers.

The dynamic dog detective kept his keen eyes open to anything out of the ordinary. Of course, *everything* at the circus was out of the ordinary.

They passed a large bright red semitrailer with gold letters on it. There was a big space between BODOLINI'S and GREATEST LITTLE BIG TOP SHOW IN THE WORLD.

Something had been painted over with red paint to match the background. With effort Sebastian could make out most of the letters. The original sign probably had said BODOLINI BROTHERS' GREATEST LITTLE BIG TOP SHOW IN THE WORLD.

So at least one sibling had co-owned this little

circus. Might he have had anything to do with Tahsha's disappearance?

Mr. Bodolini nodded toward some big cages that lined their path. "Don't get too close. The cats can reach right through the bars. And those chimps are an ill-tempered lot, too."

Cats? Sebastian knew about circus dogs, but circus cats?

Rrrrrrrrroar! A tawny lion with a shaggy mane and yellow eyes glared at Sebastian.

Oh, *those* kinds of cats. If Sebastian had been anything but the superior canine that he was, he might have tucked tail and run. He would hate to face such a cat without bars between them.

"There," Mr. Bodolini said. "That's where we kept Tahsha."

Sebastian surveyed the scene. Straw was scattered everywhere, along with peanut shells, stalks of celery, heads of lettuce, and various fruits. Tahsha didn't get to finish her supper last night.

The water trough was overturned. Was that a sign of struggle? Sebastian wondered.

Tahsha's tutu and headdress were folded neatly into an opened trunk, but her body paints were spilled all over the ground. Tahsha had stepped in the paint! Until the paint wore off, it would be a

14

cinch to follow her movements. Too bad the kidnapper hadn't stepped in the paint, too.

The steel leg band from Tahsha's leg lay open on the ground.

John pointed to a large bucket of dust nearby. "What's that for?"

Mr. Bodolini stooped to turn the water trough right side up. "For dust baths. Elephants' hides get dry and cracked in the sun. The animals cool themselves by flapping their big ears like fans, spraying water or dust over themselves, or rolling in the mud. We keep all the options available for our star performer."

Using his ballpoint pen, John carefully lifted the leg band and slipped it into a plastic bag. "One of the lab technicians will pick this up." He placed a sticker on it: Crime Scene Evidence. Do Not Touch.

Examining the band through the clear plastic, John said, "This ankle band doesn't look tampered with. If someone had forced it open, there would be scratches."

Mr. Bodolini shrugged. "We've never locked Tahsha's chain. After all, most people are afraid to come near her."

While John was marking off the area with his Do Not Cross Police Line tape, Sebastian followed the colorful footprints. He was stunned to discover that they went right up to the wire fence, where they stopped abruptly.

Mr. Bodolini had said that Tahsha was a remarkably talented elephant. But he'd never mentioned that she could fly!

3

The Purloined Pachyderm

Sebastian sat on his haunches and stared up at the fence. It was at least eight feet high. Even if elephants could climb, there were no toeholds big enough. Tahsha's feet were as big as some tree stumps. Tahsha weighed six tons. The fence would have been crushed beneath her weight.

Sebastian noticed a shoe print, too, a really huge one that overlaid the elephant prints. Despite the size, the shallowness of its impression meant that its owner couldn't weigh more than one hundred and ten, one hundred and twenty pounds.

John and Mr. Bodolini came up. "Look, your dog has the scent," Mr. Bodolini said.

John laughed. "Sebastian is on the scent of something edible, I think. He's no tracking dog. He's a couch and kitchen dog."

Humpt! A dog detective works best when he's not distracted by an empty stomach. Sebastian put his nose into the air and stalked toward the commissary, where some of the circus people were eating breakfast.

Slipping under a table, Sebastian gulped down bits of egg and Canadian bacon. He kept an ear tuned to the talk. After all, a large part of detective work was listening.

"These eggs have been watered down, and the coffee's from yesterday's grounds," a woman grumbled. "Why risk my neck on the trapeze for watery eggs and no money? If Nick doesn't pay me soon, I'm leaving. Then where will he be?"

"Broke, just like he is now," a man said. "The circus has lost its magic for people. Oh, there are a couple of big ones, but only a few of us little tent shows are left."

Sebastian scooted out of the way of shifting feet as the man continued lecturing the woman.

"Since the breakup, we're not bringing in enough money to cover our pay and maintain the animals."

The super sleuth's ears cocked forward. Breakup? What breakup?

"Peg, it's important for Nick to spend what he gets on the animals' food and vet bills." He laughed.

"You risk *your* neck? What about *me* facing those cats day after day? I sure don't want them to be *hungry*."

"All the same, I'll go somewhere else."

"You thinking of *Ringling*? They've got trapeze acts, but no one's leaving the acts."

"Well, what about Marc's circus?"

"You'd go with Nick's brother? That's disgusting. If it wasn't for him, this circus would be at least breaking even. I'll bet Marc isn't doing any better. Two halves aren't as good as a whole."

Sebastian crept away. So the other half of the Bodolini Brothers was Marc. And apparently he had a competing circus. Interesting. Also, the breakup might not have been a friendly one.

What if there were jealousy between the two brothers? Marc might have that motive for ruining this little circus. Also, Nick Bodolini was broke. What if he had insured the elephant for a lot of money? Desperation sometimes made people do bad things.

Sebastian found an insurance scam hard to believe. After all, Nick had said that Tahsha was the most important act in his circus. If Nick had stolen his own elephant, he would have had to have a better reason. But what?

John and Nick came in. They poured themselves

cups of coffee. Sebastian joined them. He looked back at the couple he'd overheard: Peg, a flame-haired woman in her thirties, maybe, and a slightly stooped, gray-haired man with a pockmarked face. Sebastian didn't know his name, but he knew he was the lion tamer. That was two people he could cross off his list of suspects, at least.

"I noticed a couple of campers parked near the fence where the footprints end," John said. "Perhaps their occupants saw or heard something that might be useful."

Nick Bodolini shook his head sadly. "We can try." He nodded toward a slender man huddled over a plate of eggs. "The cream-colored camper belongs to him, Horace, the Human Cannonball."

"The Human Cannonball?" John asked, his eyebrows raised questioningly.

"Twice a day Monday through Friday and three times a day on Saturday and Sunday, Horace is shot out of a cannon into a net at the other end of the tent."

John walked over to Horace. "I'm Detective Jones with CPD. Did you hear anything last night?"

"*What?* I can't hear you," Horace said.

Mr. Bodolini cupped his hands around his mouth and shouted, "Horace! Remove the earplugs!"

Turning to John, he said, "Sometimes he forgets. He says there's nothing much worth hearing around here, anyway."

Horace shook his head vigorously, the way Sebastian did when he was throwing off water. "Tahsha, missing?" he asked.

Sebastian crossed Horace off the suspect list, too.

"What about the other camper?" John asked Mr. Bodolini. "Who does that belong to?"

"Rambling Rose, our clown," Mr. Bodolini said.

Maybe they were getting somewhere at last.

John said, "Is that her real name, or her professional name?"

Mr. Bodolini admitted, "I never thought to ask her."

John knocked on the camper door. "Hello?" he called out. "Rambling—er, Miss Rose!"

A man in white tights and house slippers strolled by. "If you're looking for Rambling, she hasn't been here since last night. She was supposed to meet me and Zena after supper. She had an idea for a routine with us on the high wire, but she didn't show. No one has seen her."

A missing elephant and now a missing clown whose camper was parked right next to the last-found tracks of the elephant.

4

Who's Clowning Around Now?

Sebastian quickly reviewed his facts. First the elephant disappears, apparently into thin air, from this nearly bankrupt circus. Now they find out that the clown hasn't been seen since last night.

Did she see and recognize the kidnapper? Did Tahsha's kidnapper take Rambling Rose, too? Or did the clown take the elephant? If so, why?

"Who looks after the elephant?" John asked. "And where is he or she?"

"Jacob Wright is her trainer and keeper," Mr. Bodolini said. "He's pretty shaken. He's out looking for her, just in case she managed to get away from her kidnappers."

Sebastian thought that Jacob and Tahsha seemed to have genuine affection for each other. What was it he had said? Something about her missing Omar and to trust him? Who was Omar? A former keeper?

Jacob probably wouldn't let any harm come to the elephant. But what about love as a motive? Perhaps he planned to put Tahsha someplace where she could be freer, like a preserve.

By the time they reached the front gate, the Mobile Crime Scene Unit had arrived.

John told Lieutenant Scully, "I cordoned off the elephant's quarters and the area around her footprints. I also bagged her leg band. Check it for prints. Check Tahsha's quarters and both sides of the fence. Fingerprint anything that's smooth enough to hold a print."

Sebastian loped ahead of John and skidded to a stop opposite to where the prints disappeared. There were no prints on that side of the fence.

The curb, however, looked newly cracked in two places, as if something really heavy had rested there. The breaks were too far apart to have been made by Tahsha. Her prints would have been close together, even considering her bulk.

Sebastian moved closer to the fence. It had flecks of orange paint on it where something must have scraped it. There were just a few flecks, but enough

to see that the color was the same orange found on most tractors, forklifts, and cranes.

Someone must have led Tahsha to the fence, where she clearly was lifted up and over it by a heavy-duty crane. The kidnapper probably used a truck to whisk her away. Why hadn't the elephant trumpeted a warning? Had her instinct to be silent during danger worked against her?

That, to Sebastian, meant this was an inside job. The culprit was either a present employee—or employer—or a former one who wasn't afraid of the elephant. It was someone who knew that Tahsha's leg iron wouldn't be locked, someone the elephant trusted. An elephant never forgets.

Sebastian felt sure that he had met or at least heard of all the prime suspects. Nick Bodolini; Jacob Wright, Tahsha's trainer; Marc Bodolini, the hotheaded brother; and Rambling Rose, the missing clown.

Where was Jacob? Was he really out looking for the elephant? Did the missing clown have anything to do with Tahsha's disappearance? Was Bodolini trying to bail out of a bad financial situation? What about Marc? He might, as the lion tamer suggested, be having financial difficulties of his own.

Officer Scully came up. "Detective Jones, we

found this in the straw in the elephant's quarters." He handed John a plastic bag.

John held the bag up to the light and examined its contents. "A red ball? One of Tahsha's toys, per- haps?"

Mr. Bodolini stepped forward, frowning. "No, not a ball," he said. "That's a clown nose."

5

It's Rose by a Nose

"You found this clown nose in the straw in Tahsha's quarters?" John asked.

"That doesn't mean anything," Mr. Bodolini said. "Rambling is crazy about that elephant. Why, she goes by Tahsha's quarters all the time, just to take her a banana or apple or some figs. Tahsha loves figs." He turned his face away from them, but his sagging shoulders told Sebastian that he was truly miserable. Sebastian moved Nick Bodolini to the foot of the suspect list, although he didn't dismiss him.

"I hope Rambling has another nose handy, since she likes to remain in character all the time. She's always in costume," Mr. Bodolini said. "I have never heard her speak, either during the act or away from it."

"Always in costume?" John asked. "You mean she is never seen without her makeup? *Never*?"

Mr. Bodolini shook his head. "I have no idea what she looks like. Whatever her reason for remaining behind her mask, it's none of my business.

"Some people join the circus to leave something behind. Here they start over. We care only who they are from that day forward. We circus people must live together nine months out of the year. The only way to do that is to respect one another's privacy."

Mr. Bodolini shoved his hands into his back pockets and stared at the ground. "Maybe I'd better tell you about the breakup."

"Breakup? What breakup?" John asked.

Sebastian sniffed with an air of superiority. If John were as observant as his clever canine partner, he'd already know these things.

"This was once the Bodolini Brothers' circus. My brother Marc and I owned it together. He wanted to bring in high-stepping dancers and a lot of fancy laser lighting. The bigger, the glitzier, the better. He said I'm old-fashioned."

Mr. Bodolini sighed. "I like this little circus. We're like family. The workers who put up the tent last night will be performing in the big top at curtain time. There are no stars—except Tahsha. And she doesn't know how special she is. I just want to make enough to pay expenses and to put my daughter through college."

Smiling, he pulled a picture from his wallet. "This is Rosalie. She's a business major. She's going to be *somebody,* not a circus bum like me."

He replaced the picture. "I had to push her into college, or she'd be right here, following the sawdust trail just like me." He sighed.

"Anyway, Marc's five years younger than me. He was too impatient to wait for his turn to run the circus. We divided the circuit and the acts. I got Tahsha and the western and southern states. Marc got Omar and the eastern and northern states. Tahsha's the smarter of the two elephants, so Marc got our clown as compensation."

Omar was another elephant! Jacob had said Tahsha was lonely for Omar. Did he plan to unite Tahsha and Omar?

"When Rambling Rose applied for a job about then," Mr. Bodolini continued, "I jumped at the chance. And she's good."

Interesting, Sebastian thought, that Rambling Rose would apply at just the right moment. Was it a coincidence?

"Were her credentials in order?" John asked.

"What did I need besides the laughter of kids? This is her first job. She was willing to work for very little money, just to build her references."

"I'd like to see your personnel files," John said.

Sebastian thought that was a good idea. He trotted alongside John and Mr. Bodolini as they made their way to the office.

Mr. Bodolini unlocked his file cabinet. He pulled the files on Jacob and Rambling Rose.

According to his file, Jacob had been with the circus from the time it was called Bodolini and Sons twenty years ago. Since African elephants live as long as fifty years, Jacob and Tahsha probably had been together all twenty years.

Sebastian leaned over John's shoulder, reading Rambling Rose's file. It said little more than her professional name and that she had no previous experience.

There was a picture of her, but in clown makeup. What was she hiding? She wore a wig of orange-red yarn in tight curls, sort of like sheepskin. Her hat looked like an inverted flowerpot with one rose that stuck straight up about a foot above it. Her right cheek was painted with a single teardrop and her left with a blooming red rose.

It was her shoes that interested Sebastian. They were huge. And they probably had made the shoe prints that were near Tahsha's. Had Rambling Rose helped someone steal Tahsha, or had she heard a noise, gone to investigate, and gotten kidnapped along with Tahsha?

Why would she be wearing her clown shoes at night? Surely she had other shoes, normal-sized ones that were more comfortable. Perhaps she had been on her way to meet the high-wire people when she saw something suspicious.

Sebastian recalled that each clown's makeup is unique: It is registered for copyright, just as books and songs are. The library was having a special exhibit in conjunction with the circus visit. Surely it would include information on clowns.

John returned the personnel files to Mr. Bodolini. He glanced at his watch. "I'm meeting my fiancée for lunch. Meanwhile, every vehicle large enough to carry an elephant is being searched," John assured him. "No plane takes off without a thorough investigation. Police are combing the woods as we speak. If Tahsha is in there, they'll find her. We'll get back your elephant and clown, sooner or later."

"If it's later rather than sooner, I'll be out of business," Mr. Bodolini said. "Whether or not we perform, we must pay the rent and utilities on this lot." He shook his head sadly. "I'll have no choice but to disband the circus."

Mr. Bodolini put his hands to his temples, frowning. "The children will be so disappointed if Tahsha isn't here tonight. And what about Rambling? Since I was a child performing on the high wire in my father's circus, the Bodolinis have never canceled a performance."

John met Maude at the park across from the building where she worked, only a block from the library. When John was with Maude, he did more looking at her than at Sebastian. Right now they were busy talking about wedding plans, and they weren't consulting him. (If they asked, he'd have to say forget it. He was not anxious to have Lady Sharon as a stepsister. Yuk!)

The weather was steamy hot. Some of the men in the park had shed their jackets and hats. The cagey canine scooted into a natty brown blazer and wide-brimmed Panama hat before scampering down to the library.

In the lobby Sebastian found a miniature circus on display. It was a replica of a circus from the 1950s. Sebastian wiggled through the crowd and peered through the glass. The elephants were no

bigger than plums but accurate in every detail. Pea-sized poodles in top hats spun on their back legs.

One of the clowns looked amazingly like Rambling Rose. Odd, Sebastian thought. Why include her in a replica of a forty-year-old circus?

Sebastian hurried on to the reference section: *C, Circus. Circus clowns.* There. Slipping the book from the shelf, he plopped it onto a reading table and pawed through it.

Aha! Rambling Rose, with a rose painted on her right cheek and a teardrop on her left. She was five feet six, born in 1929, and famous for her solo performances. Why would she have told Mr. Bodolini that she had no experience? Was she hiding something terrible about her past?

The library had posted the year's schedules for all the circuses. Marc's circus was now in the neighboring state. It would have been possible for him to slip across the border and steal Tahsha. Since he had worked with the circus for many years, Tahsha knew him and wouldn't be afraid of him. He was a good suspect.

Perhaps he wanted to bankrupt his brother. With Nick bankrupt, Marc could reunite all the Bodolini performers in one circus—his own.

Sebastian raced back to the park. He quickly

shook himself loose from the blazer and Panama. Their owner, still deeply absorbed in working a crossword puzzle, didn't notice.

As Sebastian skidded to a halt near the park bench, John crumpled the bag Maude had brought from one of the fast-food places.

John glanced up. "Sebastian, I'm proud of you. You didn't beg for one little morsel. Here is your reward." He held out a bite-sized piece of meat. Sebastian snapped it up quickly. Such a tiny treat. *Humpt!*

Sebastian leaped into the car beside his human, eager to get back on the case.

John called Chief on his car phone. "Has anyone located Marc Bodolini yet?" John asked. "You think maybe he's here, Chief? Yes sir, I know that's my job to find out, not yours."

John turned the car south. That wasn't the way to the circus. Where was he going?

"Well, old fellow, I know you'll be glad to go home to air-conditioning."

Home! Just as the case was getting really interesting?

6

A Rose Is a Rose,
or Is It?

Sebastian sulked all the way home. He wanted to stay on the case until it had been solved. Besides, the exterminator had been at the house. It probably smelled bad, or had yucky dead bugs lying around.

When John took him inside, he coughed and sneezed and made gagging noises. Surely that would convince John that the house was not safe to enter.

John sniffed. "I think you're just being silly, Sebastian. This air is perfectly clear, and I'll leave a window open a little." He patted Sebastian on the head. "I've got to get back to work, so just settle down."

He left without another word. Sebastian stood with his nose pressed against the window, solemnly watching John pull away. Let that pathetic image in John's rearview mirror haunt him all afternoon. *Humpf!*

Sebastian trotted into the kitchen and overturned the recycling bin. Pawing through the newspapers, he pulled out the entertainment section and shook it free. There was an article about the circus, with pictures of a few of the acts.

It had a little about Rambling Rose. It called her petite, youthful, and agile. But a "petite" person was no taller than around five feet two. Yet the directory said Rambling Rose was five feet six. It also said she was born in 1929. That would make her more than sixty, hardly "youthful."

Was this Rambling Rose an impostor? First, she didn't fit the description in the official directory. Second, she never took off her makeup, which told Sebastian that she was hiding something. Third, she disappeared about the same time as the elephant. Certainly she was the four-on-the-floor detective's prime suspect.

Find her, and he'd find Tahsha, he believed. It was now several hours till the private performance. If Rambling didn't show up then, he could be pretty sure that she was somehow involved, if not as the kidnapper, at least as a covictim. If she did show up, he would follow her right to the elephant. But what about Jacob? What had he meant when he told Tahsha to trust him?

Sebastian tapped the television remote control with his paw. The set buzzed momentarily, then the picture came on. It was a "Lassie" rerun. *Humpt.* That dog had nothing on him. Besides, he'd read that there had been not one Lassie but many dogs playing the role, each with his own tricks. What a disgrace! He, Sebastian (Super Sleuth), on the other hand, would make a wonderful television star: Dashing and derring-do, and best of all, one of a kind.

Just as Lassie came face-to-face with a bear, the episode stopped and a news brief came on.

"Police are baffled by the break-in at the city zoo last night, in which nothing was taken. The front-gate padlock had been forced open. The night watchman, alerted by the noises of the disturbed animals, reported seeing the silhouettes of two people racing from the premises. He believes he frightened them away before they could do any harm. The mayor blamed the incident on the budget cuts, which forced him to lay off a second watchman."

This was not a week for animals, Sebastian thought. Might the two intruders be the ones who stole Tahsha? Were they on some sort of animal kidnapping rampage? Had he been wrong all along to think it had been an inside job?

Assuming that Tahsha's disappearance had been

noticed soon after her kidnapping, Chief had quickly cordoned off the city. The culprits couldn't have left town with her. Might she be nearby? What about empty warehouses in the area? Where could one hide something that big and potentially noisy?

Sebastian turned off the TV and pushed at the doggie door. It was locked. So much for the easy way out. He ambled into the guest bedroom. Sure enough, John had left the window slightly open to air it out. Sebastian stuck his nose under the window and pushed up. *Ooof!*

The screen was latched, but a little pawing loosened it. Sebastian squeezed through the opening and tumbled onto the ground.

He shook off the grass and leaves that clung to his shaggy fur, then loped off in the direction of the circus.

A quick survey of the neighborhood warehouses proved fruitless. Sebastian raced to the circus lot. The front gate was crowded with giggling, squealing children as they pushed toward the big top. He slipped in among them and past the guards.

He needed a disguise, but what? Spotting an open door in one of the campers, he dashed inside. The blinds were drawn, so the light was dim. His eyes adjusted quickly. Ah, there was a nice disguise:

Khaki pants and shirt, calf-high brown boots, and a jaunty helmet.

Wiggling into the outfit, Sebastian squinted through the dimness at his image in the full-length mirror. Such a dashing doggie!

Just as Sebastian turned to leave, the door flew open. The bright sunlight outlined the silhouette of a slightly stooped man. He stepped inside the door and fumbled for the light switch, clicking it several times. It failed to come on, much to Sebastian's relief.

Before Sebastian could dodge him, the man stepped forward and tumbled head over feet across the crouching dog, bumping his head.

Sebastian licked the man's cheek. When he got no response, the concerned canine put his nose near the man's. Thank goodness, he was still breathing; he was just knocked out.

Mr. Bodolini stuck his head inside the door. "Hurry, Grimsley! The acrobats are almost done."

Grateful that Mr. Bodolini had not seen Grimsley, Sebastian did as he was told. Which one was Grimsley? What did he do at the circus? Perhaps he was the man Sebastian had seen with the horses. Sebastian figured he could handle horses. He couldn't keep the kids waiting.

Bodolini opened the tent flap and once again

urged Sebastian to hurry. "There's your music! They're already in the cage!"

Sebastian raced down the canvas tunnel, which concealed his entrance into the arena. Emerging into the spotlights, he was blinded momentarily. He acknowledged the cheering crowd with a nod of his head.

Suddenly, hot sour breath struck Sebastian's face. As his vision cleared, the derring-do dog found himself face-to-face with a tawny, maned lion. The confounded canine swallowed hard. *Ulp!*

"Your whip!" someone whispered. "You forgot your whip!" It was Rambling Rose. She had returned for the performance, and she *could* speak.

From the corner of his eye, Sebastian saw John motioning for Rambling to come to him. She seemed to be heading in the opposite direction, however. Sebastian couldn't help his buddy. The dynamic dog had his own problems.

Sebastian had seen circuses on TV. The lion tamer cracked his whip in the air or on the floor, and the cats did tricks. Unfortunately, that took practice.

Dropping the whip, Sebastian leaped atop a perch and howled for John. *Ahrooooooo!* It sounded a little like the Tarzan yell.

The lion leaped onto the perch with him and

roared. Sebastian took a deep breath. His brain needed oxygen; he needed to think! The man had said that his cats were well fed. That was good; they wouldn't be hungry. Also, he remembered reading that the females do all the hunting, while the male cats rest in the shade. The huge manes on these cats meant that they were males, so they were not likely to take him down themselves.

There was not enough room for Sebastian and the lion on this perch, and the lion didn't seem inclined to give up his space. Sebastian leaped to the next, higher perch. The lion followed him, and a second lion leaped onto the first perch. These old cats knew the routine so well that they could do it without any coaxing from him.

As cheers and whistles erupted from the audience, Sebastian jumped from the perch, stretched out his front paws, and dipped his chin all the way to the floor in a bow. Then he spun around and raced back down the canvas tunnel before the big cats could change their minds.

"Great job tonight!" Mr. Bodolini shouted as Sebastian exited the canvas tunnel. "Good touch, throwing away the whip and giving that jungle yell!"

Sebastian scampered toward Grimsley's camper. He noticed Rambling's hat and wig lying near her

camper's door. She must have exited in a hurry.

At Grimsley's camper, the tamer was stirring but still groggy. The hairy hawkshaw shook himself out of the man's clothes. Enough of that! He would find something with sequins on it instead. Surely someone wearing sequins wasn't doing anything dangerous.

Scudding along the line of campers, he pushed at the doors until one gave. Inside he found billowy pantaloons, a sequined top with puffy sleeves, and a tall, glittery hat with a veil big enough to cover his face.

He had to find Rambling. He had to see if she would lead him to the elephant. Whatever she was hiding behind that clown mask, she had found the perfect disguise. Who would suspect a clown among a bunch of circus people? It would be like hiding a tree inside a forest. Or—

Of course! How could he have been so dense! Where do you hide an elephant? The answer was crystal clear. If he was right, he would have Tahsha back before her act was scheduled to go on. The children were waiting.

The hideout was less than a mile from here. That would explain why no one heard the getaway. At night, at this end of town, with the workers hammering away in the big top, it was easy to cover the crime.

Reaching the zoo, Sebastian knocked over a couple of trash cans outside the gate to distract the guard, then scudded in as quickly as he could. Past the hippos, past the giraffes he ran. Time was running out.

At the elephant stockade, the sign said that the animals' names were Tonga, Raffa, Ruby, Mata, and Snarbu. Sebastian rose onto the fence and peered inside. He counted one, two, three, four, five—six elephants.

The sixth elephant confirmed his suspicion. The kidnapper had hidden her before everyone's eyes, right there in the zoo. Sebastian wished he could yell, *Tahsha, come!* But all that came out was a throaty *Wahroof!*

One of the elephants raised her trunk and gave out a mighty trumpet. The others joined in. The first one came over to the fence. She rose up on her hind legs and trumpeted once more. Then she shook her back end in something like a hula dance. It was Tahsha!

7

A Rose by
Any Other Name

Tahsha had remembered the old sleuth, just as Jacob had said she would. But how could he get her out of here and back to the circus?

A little boy who was standing nearby yelled, "Mommy, Daddy, look! Look at that trick elephant!"

"In a minute, dear," a woman called back in a singsong voice. "We're watching the seals right now. See how cute they are, clapping their fins?"

Sebastian pawed at the gate latch. The little boy grinned. He put his finger to his lips. "*Shhh,* don't tell," he said. He lifted the latch.

Tahsha lumbered through the gate. The other elephants came out, too. They strolled calmly along the walkways, snapping twigs off the hedges as they went. People screamed, and elephants scattered. The zookeeper and his helpers scrambled after them, trying to herd them back behind the stockade.

Tahsha wrapped her trunk around Sebastian's body. She scooped him up onto her broad, flat head. He didn't have to tell her where to go. She remembered.

As everyone was inside the big top watching the circus, the midway was empty. Sebastian urged Tahsha forward, and she ambled into the big top with Sebastian still perched atop her head.

"And so, boys and girls," Mr. Bodolini was saying as he pressed Tahsha's empty tutu to his chest, "it is my sad duty to tell you that Tahsha will not—"

Ahwaaaaaaahaaa! Tahsha gave a mighty trumpet.

Mr. Bodolini looked up and grinned. "I mean, it's my *happy* duty to introduce Tahsha!"

Jacob, his eyes glistening with tears, rushed forward and rubbed her trunk with his cheek. Tahsha wrapped her trunk around his neck in a caress. Then Jacob called out commands, and Tahsha hula danced, twisted, and sat on Jacob without hurting him at all, all with Sebastian riding her. The children laughed and shouted with delight.

Sebastian bowed humbly. It was easy to be humble when there were several puzzling aspects of the mystery left unsolved.

Who had taken Tahsha? And who was Rambling Rose? More important, *where* was Rambling Rose?

Sebastian scrambled down and raced to Rambling's camper. He peered inside. She wasn't there. Something peculiar *was* there, however, sitting on her dressing table. It was a picture of Tahsha in her tutu, with Mr. Bodolini.

Why would Rambling Rose have a picture of Tahsha on her dressing table? He was convinced that she was somehow involved, although he didn't have a clue as to why or how to prove it.

Sebastian hurried to the area where the circus performers were signing autographs for the children. A petite young woman whom Sebastian recognized as Mr. Bodolini's daughter was the last in the ringmaster's line.

Mr. Bodolini looked up. "Rosalie! Aren't you supposed to be in class?"

"Dad, we have to talk," Rosalie said.

"Of course, honey. I always listen to my girl."

"But you *don't* listen, Dad. I told you I didn't want to be a business major. I didn't want to go to college. I wanted to be in the circus. It's in my blood, too, you know."

"And I told you that you had to go to college,"

he said. "There's nothing that you can do in the circus."

Sebastian noticed the slightest smear of greasepaint on her sleeve. Pretending to stumble, he pushed against Rosalie. She dropped her purse. Its contents tumbled onto the autograph table. There were several tubes of greasepaint.

Rosalie picked up the red. Without a mirror she drew a rose on her cheek. With the blue she drew a tear on the other. He was right. Rambling Rose, Rosalie: They were one and the same. Had she disguised herself as a clown to steal the elephant from her own father? Because he had made her go to college?

Mr. Bodolini stared, openmouthed. "You—you're Rambling Rose, my clown?"

"I knew that if you didn't know you would judge my act fairly. I read in *Variety* that Rambling Rose had retired, so I called her. She agreed to let me use her design, as long as I reversed the rose and tear. I thought surely you would guess, but you never did."

"And when were you going to tell me?"

"When the season was over."

"It's over for you now," Mr. Bodolini said angrily. "You are to go back to college this instant!"

"And disappoint the kids? Not a chance," Rosalie said. "Besides, you need me. Uncle Marc has your old clown, remember?"

"Don't remind me!" Mr. Bodolini said.

Rosalie rolled her eyes. "Oh, you two! What if I told you he's here, Dad. He's ready to reunite the two halves of the circus, make it the Bodolini Brothers, the way it should be."

It was now clear to the hairy hawkshaw: Marc Bodolini, with Rosalie's knowledge or even her help, had taken Tahsha. His motive was not to ruin Nick but to make him anxious to have a single Bodolini circus again.

Rosalie motioned into the crowd, and a man who looked like a younger version of Nick came forward. From the hug the two brothers gave each other, Sebastian figured all was forgiven.

There was still the matter, however, of a kidnapped elephant and breaking and entering the zoo that Marc (and his accomplices, if any) had to answer for. But how could the sleuth prove it?

Of course, an elephant never forgets. Perhaps he could get Tahsha to help.

Sebastian hurried to Tahsha's quarters. He pulled at Jacob's sleeve, trying to get him to understand. He didn't understand, but Tahsha did. She swayed back and forth. She curled and uncurled her trunk, and she flapped her winglike ears and cried out a loud *Ahwaaaaaaahaaa!*

Nick Bodolini, with Marc following closely, rushed to her. "What's the matter with Tahsha?" Nick yelled.

Tahsha curled her trunk around Marc and sat him on the ground with a plop. Then she turned her big body around and sat on him. She was careful not to hurt him, but he couldn't get up.

John arrived, breathless. "Mr. Bodolini, I have a lead on your elephant's whereabouts!" he said. "I think the zoo intruders were actually stowing her th— Oh! I see that she's back. Well, I think I know who took her. It was your bro—" Pausing, John nodded toward Marc, who was still squirming beneath Tahsha. "Er, your brother?"

Mr. Bodolini sighed. "I'm afraid so."

Jacob tapped Tahsha with his guide stick. "Up, Tahsha!"

When Marc was free, he stood looking at his feet. "I didn't mean any harm. I wouldn't hurt Tahsha or my brother. When Jacob wrote about how lonely Tahsha was and how poorly the circus was doing, I had to do something. Omar is lonely, too. He doesn't want to perform without Tahsha. I thought if it looked like I was the one to find her, Nick would be so grateful that he'd take me back, no questions asked."

"And I saw the whole thing," Rosalie said.

That explained the clown nose found in the straw, Sebastian figured.

"When Uncle Marc told me his plan, I agreed to keep quiet for twenty-four hours. But we didn't break into the zoo, honest! The front gate was open!"

Satisfied that the mystery had been solved, Sebastian slipped from the crowd. He returned the costume and raced to beat John home.

Eventually the night watchman, at first believed to be a hero for thwarting a crime, admitted that he had forgotten to lock up. So Marc was charged with entering the zoo without a ticket but not with breaking in. Since Rosalie did not actually go inside the gates, she was not charged at all.

He and Rosalie were soundly reprimanded by the judge for costing the city so much for the needless search. However, the publicity attracted people to the circus from all around the state. For a change, the circus made a tidy profit. The city, which collected plenty of taxes on the sale of food, lodging, and souvenirs, dropped the charges and ignored the fines.

Several months later, while John sat with Maude reading the newspaper announcement of their approaching marriage, Sebastian caught sight of an article on the back. It told of the rejoining of the two Bodolini circuses. It said that Rosalie Bodolini had returned to college to complete her studies. When she was graduated, she would handle the business side of the circus and perform as a clown.

The lion tamer had changed his act to exclude whips. "That first night I did it is a blur, due to a slight accident. However, I'm told I was magnificent. So how can I do less now?" he said.

There was a picture of Tahsha and Omar, their trunks entwined in a happy hug. The article credited a mysterious stranger in a circus harem costume with returning Tahsha.

Sebastian made a chuckling grunt deep in his throat. It might be a mystery to the humans, but Tahsha knew. After all, an elephant, like the clever canine detective who had rescued her, never forgets.